To Spence and Dylan, a dauntless duo —A. S.

For Simon, Mo, Cathy and Tom —D. P.

Book design by Kristen M. Nobles and Kristine Brogno.
Typeset in Cheltenham and Corndog.
The illustrations for this book were rendered in acrylic and alkyd paints and pencil.
Manufactured in Hong Kong.

Library of Congress Cataloging-in-Publication Data
Schertle, Alice.
The adventures of old Bo Bear / by Alice Schertle ; illustrated by David Parkins.
p. cm.
Summary: After his toy bear comes out of the washing machine with an ear missing
and not smelling "right," a boy takes him outside to play until he looks
and smells familiar once again.
ISBN-13: 978-0-8118-3476-6
ISBN-10: 0-8118-3476-X
[1. Cleanliness—Fiction. 2. Teddy bears—Fiction. 3. Play—Fiction. 4. Stories in rhyme.]
I. Parkins, David, ill. II. Title.
PZ8.3.S335Ad 2005
[E]—dc22
2004021581

Distributed in Canada by Raincoast Books
9050 Shaughnessy Street
Vancouver, British Columbia V6P 6E5

10 9 8 7 6 5 4 3 2 1

Chronicle Books LLC
85 Second Street
San Francisco, California 94105

www.chroniclekids.com

THE ADVENTURES OF OLD BO BEAR

chronicle books · san francisco

By Alice Schertle ★ Illustrated by David Parkins

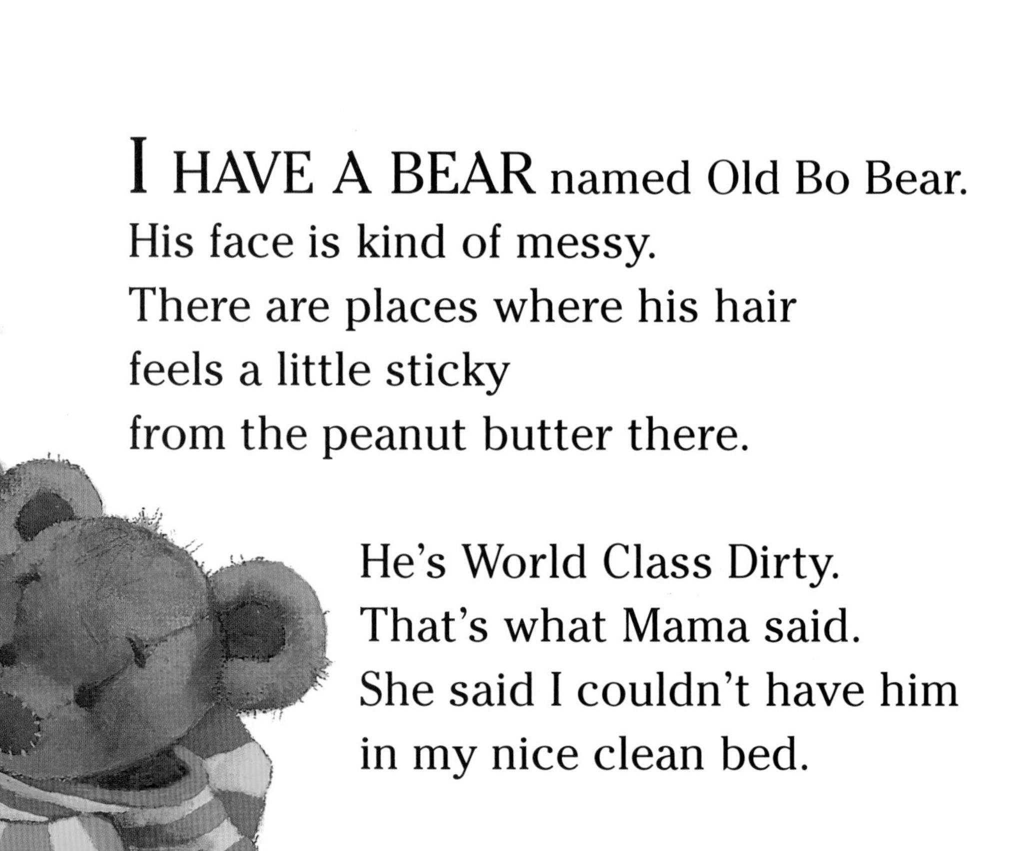

I HAVE A BEAR named Old Bo Bear.
His face is kind of messy.
There are places where his hair
feels a little sticky
from the peanut butter there.

He's World Class Dirty.
That's what Mama said.
She said I couldn't have him
in my nice clean bed.

She took him to the laundry with the dirty clothes,
opened up the washer and said, “In he goes!”

Socks, and shirts, and underwear,
pink pajamas, and Old Bo Bear
turned and tumbled, slished and sloshed,
with bubbles and suds—
and came out washed.

I dried Bo off and held him tight.
He looked all fluffy. He didn't smell right.
And an awful thing happened when Bo got clean—
He lost one ear in the washing machine!

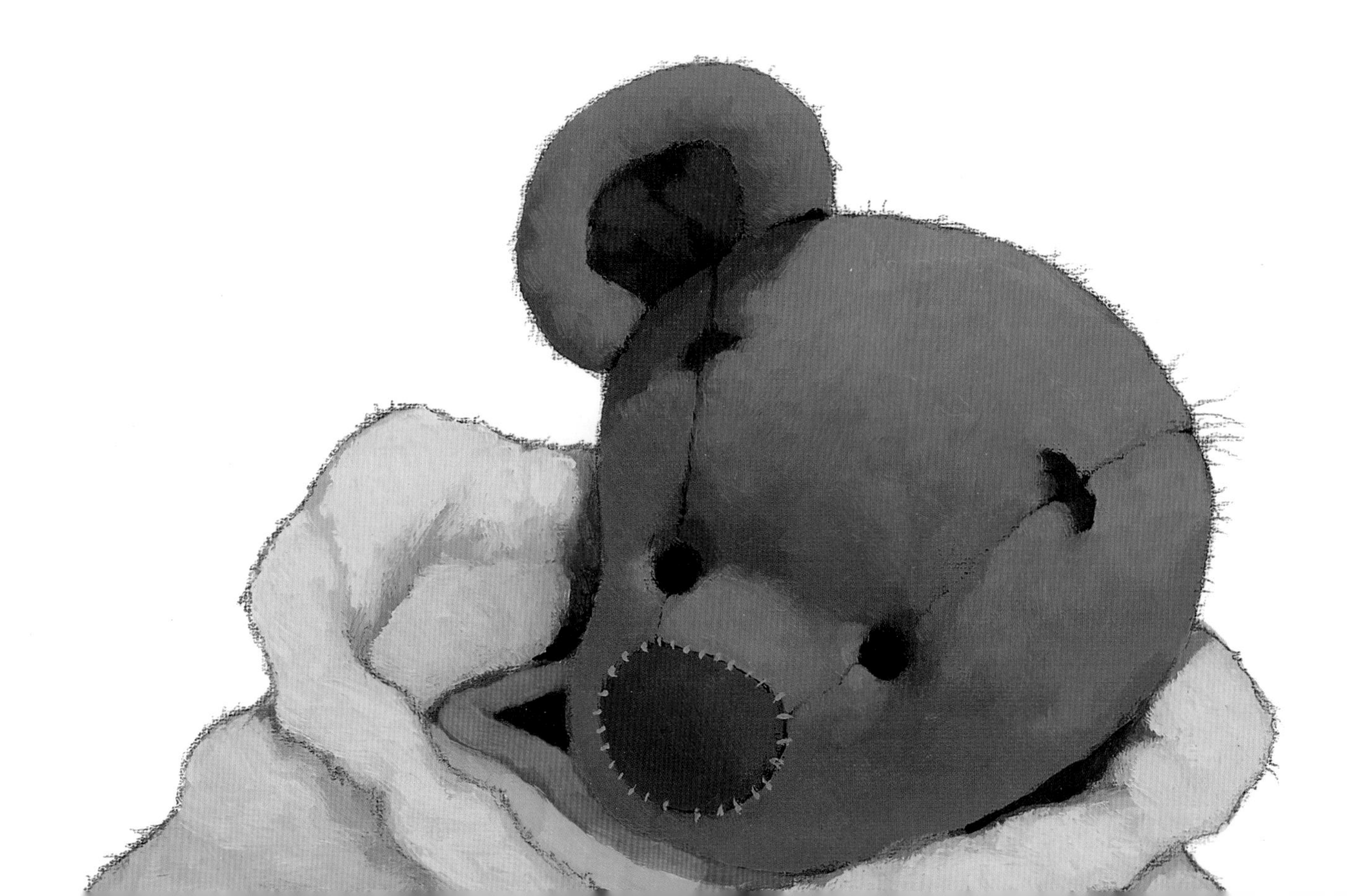

I packed provisions for Bo and me,
and we crawled in under the willow tree.
We took a map, a blue balloon,
some chocolate syrup, and a wooden spoon.

I said, "We're safe." Bo said, "I *hope*."
We both kept watch through a telescope.
We had syrup in a spoon; it tasted fine.
Bo spilled his and I spilled mine.

I was Captain Guts and Bo was Scar.
We were two bad pirates and mean as tar.
Scar lost his ear in a pirate fight.
He looked like a salty old bear, all right.

Then we saddled a pony and we rode out West.
We said I was Dakota. Bo was the best
bronco buster from far or near.
He was bucked off once and he lost an ear,
but he just said, "Shucks, that's one ear gone."
And he kind of grinned, and he climbed back on.

I was the sheriff of a Wild West town.
Deputy Bear and I rode down
Ambush Canyon on the outlaws' trail.
We roped the varmints and clapped 'em in jail.

The town turned out to wave good-bye.
We rode into the sunset, Bo and I.

Then we ran next door to the vacant lot,
and we dug some dirt, and we moved some rock,
and we made some roads and a big rock wall.
We didn't try to stay clean at all.

We said my name was Pete and Bo was Bob.
We said he lost his ear on a construction job.
We were World Class Dirty and we didn't care.
And Bo was looking like my Old Bo Bear.

So we snuck in the house like a couple of spies.
We peeked in the kitchen. We were private eyes:
Agent X and Bo, The Ear.
We dashed upstairs when the coast was clear.

Now Bo's in my backpack
where he can't be seen.
And he's *not*
going back
in the washing machine.